MARION DANE BAUER

Little Dog, Lost

with illustrations by JENNIFER A. BELL

D0586234

Atheneum Books for Young Readers
New York London Toronto Sydney New Delhi

ATHENEUM BOOKS FOR YOUNG READERS

An imprint of Simon & Schuster Children's Publishing Division

1230 Avenue of the Americas, New York, New York 10020

Text copyright © 2012 by Marion Dane Bauer

Illustrations copyright © 2012 by Jennifer A. Bell

For information about special discounts for bulk purchases, please contact Simon & Schuster Special Sales at 1-866-506-1949 or business@simonandschuster.com.

The Simon & Schuster Speakers Bureau can bring authors to your live event. For more information or to book an event, contact the Simon & Schuster Speakers Bureau at 1-866-248-3049 or visit our website at www.simonspeakers.com.

Book design by Lauren Rille

The text for this book is set in Perpetua.

The illustrations for this book are rendered in pencil and finished digitally.

Manufactured in the United States of America

0312 FFG

First Edition

10 9 8 7 6 5 4 3 2 1

Library of Congress Cataloging-in-Publication Data

Bauer, Marion Dane.

Little dog, lost / Marion Dane Bauer ; illustrated by Jennifer Bell. — 1st ed.

p. cm.

ISBN 978-1-4424-3423-3 (hardcover)

ISBN 978-1-4424-3425-7 (eBook)

[1. Novels in verse. 2. Loneliness—Fiction. 3. Dogs—Fiction. 4. Parks—Fiction. 5. City and town life—Fiction.] I. Bell, Jennifer A., ill. II. Title.

PZ7.5.B385Li 2012

[Fic]—dc23 2011034024

In memory of Ruby,
beloved service dog for Martha Bird
and the model—
especially through the ears—
for Buddy
—M. D. B.

For my two Valentines
—J. A. B.

Acknowledgments

My appreciation to Rubin Pfeffer
of East/West Literary Agency, who found my lost little dog
a home and then watched over her with such loving care.

And to Kiley Frank of Atheneum,
who helped me find the story I most wanted to write.

And to Ariel Colletti of Atheneum,
who finished the journey with Buddy and me.

And, of course, to Dawn, my ruby Cavalier,
who lay under my desk patiently, day after day, waiting for
this latest competitor for my attention to come to life . . .
or at least for me to leave the competitor behind
and go for a walk.

—M. D. B.

Little dog,
lost.
Little black dog with brown paws
and a brown mask
and a sweet ruffle of brown fur on her bum
just beneath her black whip of a tail.
Satiny coat.
Ears like airplane wings
that drop
just at the tips.
She used to be called Buddy
until no one called her anything at all.
"Hey, you!" maybe.
Or "Shoo!"
Names to run from.

Buddy wasn't always lost.
Once she owned a boy.
It was the boy who named her.
("I know she's a girl," he'd say,
"but she's my buddy anyway.")
Her boy threw a ball
again
and again

and again
until Buddy flopped
onto her belly
in the tickling grass
and dropped
the ball
between her paws,
her tongue as limp
as
a
dishrag
Come and get it, her grin always said,
and then I'll chase some more.

The boy used to take Buddy's pointy face
between his hands
and kiss her on the lips,
just like that.
When Buddy was quick,
she could get in a lick
at the exact moment
of the kiss.
The boy would say, "Arghhh!"
and wipe his mouth
· with the back of his hand.

Then he'd kiss Buddy

on the lips
again.

In short,
Buddy and her boy
were perfectly matched
and perfectly happy
together.
But nothing,
not even the sweetest love,
can be certain
of lasting
forever.

2

Not every boy
has the good fortune
of growing up
with a dog to love.
Another boy—
his name was Mark—
in another town—
the town was named Erthly—
had no dog
at all.
Mark had wanted a dog

for as long as he could remember.
He had asked for a dog.
He had begged for a dog.
He had pleaded and prayed and whined for a dog.
Once he'd even tried barking for a dog.
All to no avail.
His mother always said, "No."
"Puppies piddle,"
she said.
"Puppies chew."
"I'm sorry, Mark,"
she said every time he asked,
"no dog!"
Though she never looked very sorry.

Mark's mother gave him much
of what he asked for:
She gave him the catcher's mitt
he'd admired in the window
of the hardware store
when it wasn't even Christmas
or his birthday.
She gave him an almost-new bike.
And just about every time
they made the long drive
into the city

she gave him money to buy
a triple-decker ice cream cone
with chocolate on the bottom
and chocolate on the top
and peppermint crunch
in the middle.
She even gave him things
he'd never asked for:
food on the table,
clothes to wear,
a nice little house
with a big green backyard
(perfect for a dog).
But no dog.

Maybe it was his mother's "No!"—
the flatness of it,
the certainty—
that made Mark want a dog
so much.
Maybe it was that,
before Mark was even born,
his father had gone out
to buy a loaf of pumpernickel bread
and had kept on going.
That's the way Mark's mother put it.

"He went out to buy a loaf of pumpernickel bread."
Mark knew it was a joke—
sort of—
but still,
he had never liked pumpernickel.
It wasn't that he missed his father.
How can you miss somebody you've never met?
But sometimes
his nice little house
and his big green backyard
and his life
seemed kind of lonely
somehow.
So Mark had decided
long ago
that a boy without a dad
or a brother
or a sister
or even a cousin
living close enough to count
needed
a
dog.

He spent hours and hours
reading about dogs.

If he ever got one of his own,
he knew
exactly
how to care for it.
You had to give a dog
food,
fresh water,
exercise,
some good work to do—
like chasing a ball for a boy—
and lots and lots of love.
Mark knew how to do all that.
No problem.
He'd even practiced.
Again and again,
in his imagination,
he'd fed his dog,
he'd talked to his dog,
he'd scratched his imaginary dog
until he'd found the spot
that made an imaginary hind leg
thump
with pleasure.
And every night
he patted the place
next to where he lay in bed

and said,
"Here you go.
Come on up now."
And the dog who lived
in his mind
always jumped
right
up.

But when he asked his mother again,
she still said,
"No!"

3

Most of Mark's friends
in the town of Erthly
had dogs.
Mark didn't mind that they had dogs
and that he didn't.
Well,
maybe he did mind,
a little,
but he didn't want their dogs
to go away.
He just wanted a dog

of his own.

Alex had a pure white German shepherd
named Blizzard.

Ryan had Cinder,
a schnoodle.
(A schnoodle,
in case you don't know,
is a cross between a schnauzer
and a poodle.)
Cinder was short
and square
and,
to be perfectly honest,
rather chubby,
just like Ryan.

Samantha had a dachshund.
His name was Hotdog.

Trent didn't have a dog.
He had a large orange-marmalade cat
named Fido.
Fido walked on a leash
like any proper dog,

and he was friends
with every dog in town too.
But that was because every dog in town
knew how to behave
around Fido:
tail down,
head down,
ears down,
eyes down.
When they approached Fido that way,
properly respectful,
he touched noses with them,
politely,
and then let them be.
However,
if a new dog came prancing by,
head and tail high,
not knowing his proper place in Erthly,
Fido hit the end of his leash
like a runaway freight train,
pulling himself free.
What followed
could have come right out of a rodeo.
Fido,
tail puffed and pointing to the sky,
rode the dog's back

the way a cowboy rides a bull.
The difference
between Fido
and the cowboy
was that Fido had more spurs.
If the new dog had merely
been exploring,
he'd never be seen in Erthly again.
If he'd come to Erthly to stay,
he would have learned his lesson.
The next time he met Fido,
he'd tuck his tail,
lower his head,
drop his ears,
cast his eyes down,
and pretend to be very interested
in a good smell
far,
far
from Fido.

Lia didn't have a dog either,
but she walked her aunt's dogs,
two golden retrievers named Polly and Daisy.
She walked them every day
for fifty cents.

Practically every one of Mark's friends
had a dog.
And they all
shared their dogs
with Mark.
But it wasn't the same,
sharing a dog,
when the leash
was attached
to someone else.

One bright summer morning
Mark woke,
thinking about dogs.
That wasn't unusual.
He often lay in bed,
listening to his mother
clink about in the kitchen
and thinking about the dog he wanted:
big or small,
rough-coated or soft,
black or brown or white or red or brindled.
This time,
though,
he found himself thinking

instead
about his friends' dogs.
He found himself thinking
how much fun it would be
to have a place in Erthly
where dogs and kids
could run free,
a place
where *he* could run free with the dogs!
"What we need in this town,"
he said,
right out loud to the light fixture
hanging above his bed,
"is a dog park."

He could see it all!
He and his friends
would step through the gate
of the dog park,
unsnap the leashes,
and watch the snarl of dogs
untangle and bound away,
scattering rabbits and squirrels
like leaves
before a rowdy breeze.
Mark's scalp,

beneath his bristle of brown hair,
tingled,
just thinking about it.

He would ask his mother.
Not for a dog this time.
He knew the answer to that.
He would ask for a dog park
instead.

His mother,
you see,
was the mayor of Erthly,
and if anyone could get them
a dog park,
she was the one.

4

Back to Buddy.
She'd had a family once.
But then you know
about her boy.
She had a mom and a dad, too.
Grandparents.
Aunts and uncles.

Cousins.
She even had a dog cousin,
a raggedy terrier named Rikki.
Buddy and Rikki used to play chase
around Rikki's backyard
whenever Buddy visited.
They'd tussle and tumble,
growl and grin,
grab each other by the scruff of the neck.
(Do you know what "scruff" means?
I'll tell you,
just in case you don't.
"Scruff" is another word for "nape."
Oops!
You don't know "nape," either?
How silly of me.
It means the *back* of the neck.
Yes, I know.
I could have said so.
But "scruff" is such a satisfying word,
don't you think?)

Scruff or nape or back of the neck,
however you name it,
Buddy was a very happy dog.

But all that was before.

Before Dad said, "We're moving."
Before Dad said, "We're moving far away."
Before he said, "We're moving
to an apartment in a big city."
Then he looked down at Buddy's airplane ears
that drooped just at the tips
and said,
"An apartment in a big city is no place for a dog.
We'll have to find a new home
for Buddy."

The boy cried.
Mom blew her nose.
Even Dad took a deep breath
and turned to look out the window.
But when he turned back
again,
he had nothing more to say.

Everything the family owned
disappeared into boxes,
except Buddy's bowl,
her bed,

her bone,
her ball,
the orange-marmalade stuffed cat she liked to toss
into the air
and
catch
again.
The orange-marmalade stuffed cat
she always rested her chin on at night
when she slept.

Everything disappeared into the moving van
or into the car.
Even Buddy piled into the car
with her bowl,
her bed,
her bone,
her ball,
and her stuffed cat.

Buddy was excited.
She loved car rides.
Maybe she was going to visit her cousin,
Rikki,
the ragged terrier.

And they did

indeed
drive to another town,
but not to the one where Rikki lived.
They drove to a town called Erthly,
though no one bothered
to tell Buddy
the town's name.
When the car stopped
in front of a strange house,
the boy got out
with Buddy on her red leash.
Mom got out too,
carrying Buddy's bowl
and bed
and bone
and ball.
Buddy carried her own
orange-marmalade stuffed cat.

A woman
with salt-and-pepper hair
opened the door of the strange house.
She looked down at Buddy,
at her airplane ears
and the sweet ruffle of brown fur
on her bum.
"I'll take good care of her,"

she said.
And then she added,
"What did you say her name was again?"
"Buddy,"
the boy and his mom said together.
"Buddy,"
the woman repeated,
like someone memorizing a difficult poem.

Then the boy gave Buddy
a scratch
behind her left ear
where she always had an itch.
And he gave her
a kiss
on the lips.

Buddy got in
one
last
lick.

And the boy and his mother
walked slowly

back to the car.

The woman waved good-bye
and shut her door.
She looked down at the little black dog
with a brown mask.
She looked at Buddy's bowl
and bed
and bone
and ball.
She looked at the orange-marmalade stuffed cat.
"Oh, my," she said.
"I know nothing about dogs.
How will we manage,
you and I?"

5

"A dog park?"
Mark's mother
turned from the eggs she was frying.
A crease dug deep
into the pale space
between her eyebrows.
"Erthly is a small town,
Mark,"

she said.
"The budget has no room
for dog parks.
We'd have to buy land.
We'd have to build a fence.
Someone would have to take care of it.
It would take too much money.
Don't you see?"

Mark didn't see.
He didn't want to see.
He refused to see
anything.
He slumped in his chair.

"The park we have
needs new playground equipment,"
his mother went on.
"Those rusty old swings are a disgrace.
And there are potholes
all up and down Walnut Street.
Besides,"
she added,
"the sheriff needs a raise."

Mark sighed.

The sheriff was Trent's dad.
It would be fine
if Trent's dad
got a raise.

Mark's mother ran a hand over the bristle
of his brown hair.
"What do you want with a dog park, anyway?"
she asked,
her voice soft.
"You don't have a dog."

But that was the point, wasn't it?
It was because Mark *didn't* have
a dog
of his own
that he *needed*
a dog park.

6

Mark got onto his bike
and rode
down the middle
of Walnut Street,
being careful

to hit every pothole
dead center.

A teenage boy
was mowing the lawn
in front of the library,
and the fragrance of cut grass
hung in the air,
heavy and sweet.
The smell made Mark think
of horses
munching.
It made him think
of dogs
running free
in a dog park.

Grown-ups used money
as an excuse
for anything
they didn't want to do.
If his mother
wanted a dog park,
she could find a way.

Mark rode up and down Walnut Street

three times,
until his teeth ached
from clacking together
when he hit the potholes.
Then he rode to the town park,
leaned his bike against a tree,
and sat
on a rusty swing.

A bee buzzed past
in the honeyed sunlight.
A woodpecker *rat-a-tat-tat*-ted
in a tree.
Squirrels chittered
and threw themselves
from branch
to branch
to branch.
Mark looked around.
This park was fine,
but they couldn't use it
to let dogs run free.
There was no fence.
And besides,
old people and little kids

hung out here.

Still . . .
there had to be a way.
Mark sat,
thinking,
twisting the swing
back and forth,
scraping his heels
in the dust.

And that was when
he remembered
something he'd seen on the news
once.
A rally.
He wasn't sure what the people
had been rallying for,
but they had made a great commotion:
chants,
signs,
speeches . . .
the works.
They had made such a commotion,
in fact,

that even the president
of the whole United States
had had to listen
to what they wanted.

What if Mark and his friends
put on a rally?
What if they demanded
a dog park
in Erthly?
They could make up chants,
signs,
speeches.
This was Wednesday.
The town council was meeting
on Thursday.
Tomorrow evening he and his friends (could) march
down the middle of Walnut Street
and right to the basement
of the Catholic Church,
where the mayor
and the town council met.
The town council
would have to listen.
His mom would too.
That was the mayor's job,

to listen.
She always said so.

Mark climbed back onto his bike
and headed out
again.
He knew exactly what to do.
He'd call a meeting.
His friends would love the idea
of a dog park.
They'd love the idea of a rally,
too.
They could meet
beneath the big oak tree
in the middle of town
to make plans.
No one ever hung out there
beneath that old tree.
It would be the perfect place
to make plans.
They could decide on signs
and chants.
They could choose someone
to lead the parade.
They could decide
who would make a speech

to the council
too!

But they had to get moving.
They didn't have much time.

7

Shall I tell you more
about the town of Erthly,
where Mark
was planning a rally?
It was a small town,
as I've already said.
Too small—
according to the mayor, anyway—
for a dog park,
too big to let the dogs run free.
Like all towns,
Erthly had good folks,
and ornery ones too.
(There were even good folks
who were sometimes ornery
and ornery ones
who were sometimes good.)

No one knew how the town had come

to be named
Erthly.
Some said the first person
who'd ever built a house
beneath the arching trees,
along the rambling river,
had been named Erthly.
But no one remembered ever meeting
a person with such a name.

Others said
the town was named Erthly
because it was
the exact center of the earth,
at least for the folks
who lived there.
But no one was sure of that,
either.

Sometimes one of the ornery folks
would say
that the town was named Erthly
for no earthly reason
and that the whole question was silly
anyway.
And after that was said,
the discussion about the town's name

always ended.

However the name Erthly had come about,
it was a small town.
No skyscrapers.
No big public buildings
with marble floors
and statues on the lawn.
Not even a traffic light.
Nonetheless,
Erthly had a school
and three churches,
a grocery store,
a library,
a post office,
a hardware store,
a bank,
Misty's hair salon
(Misty did nails, too),
a drugstore,
a café,
and two gas stations
right across the street from each other.

It also had a park with rusty swings,
potholes along the length of Walnut Street,

and a sheriff who needed a raise
because his wife had recently had a baby.
But those things you already know . . .
except about the baby.

There is something else I haven't told you,
however.
At the exact center
of Erthly
stood a very large house.
You might even call it a mansion.
It had a round tower
with a roof
like a witch's hat.
It also had
big double doors with
lion's-head knockers,
the kind where the knockers
pass through the lions' noses.
(An odd concept,
if you think about it.)
Stained-glass windows
flanked the big double doors.
And to reach the doors
or knockers
or stained-glass windows,

you passed
between fat white columns
and crossed a broad porch.

An expanse of lawn
surrounded the house.
A tall iron fence
enclosed the lawn.
The fence had spikes
at frequent intervals,
so even the most daring boys
rarely climbed it
to investigate the lawn
or to tiptoe
across the broad porch
and pluck at
a lion's nose
or to peek
through the stained-glass windows.

And I mustn't forget to mention
the enormous oak tree
just outside
the fence.
It was the oldest,
the tallest,

the grandest
tree in town,
but folks rarely paused there
beneath its branches.
Perhaps that had something to do
with the mansion,
the lion's-head knockers,
and the tall iron fence
with spikes.
Or maybe it had to do
with Charles Larue,
the old caretaker
who had lived alone
in the house
for many years.
He had stayed on
after the lady who'd owned the house
had gone missing.

Neither the good folks in town
nor the ornery ones
could agree
about what had happened
to the lady.
Some thought she had moved to Hawaii,
where the weather was always warm

and whales
frolicked in the sea.
Others said she had gone
to a nursing home
in a town nearby.
Some were sure she had died.
The last time they'd seen her,
she'd been very old,
after all.

Though Charles Larue
still lived in the mansion
in the exact center of Erthly,
no one had ever asked him
about his lady.
Maybe they were afraid
to talk to a man
who lived in a mansion.
Or perhaps they didn't speak
because Charles Larue
was the quietest man
any of them had ever known . . .
or not known,
as the case may be.
He was so quiet
that folks were certain

he was snooty . . .
or perhaps even mean.

He lived in a mansion,
didn't he—
while the rest of them lived
in ordinary houses?
Surely that was proof of something!

Charles Larue was a small man,
no one to be afraid of,
really.
Unless you were afraid
of the great bush of his white eyebrows
or the great beak of his nose.
But to be afraid of those,
you had to ignore
the sweet, sad eyes
between eyebrows and nose,
eyes as blue as a Caribbean sea.
And you had to forget
the way Charles Larue walked
when he emerged from the house,
hands thrust deep into his pockets,
head bowed
as though against a bitter wind

even on the sunniest summer day.
And you had to pretend
you didn't notice
the shy way he glanced up
and then away again
when anyone came near.

It's amazing,
though,
what folks can ignore,
forget,
pretend.
So every Saturday morning
when Charles Larue
unlocked the gate
in the iron fence
with spikes
and walked up Walnut Street
to Stanley's Grocery Store,
everyone in Erthly watched,
but no one spoke
and no one came near.

Thus in silence
Charles Larue selected his groceries

and set them
in front of Mrs. Stanley,
the grocer:
a dozen eggs,
bread,
peanut butter,
an apple or two,
several cans of baked beans,
and one large Milky Way candy bar.
He paid with wrinkled bills
pulled from deep inside his pocket,
along with a smattering of coins.
And, carrying his bag of groceries,
he walked back
up the street,
pushed through the gate in the iron fence with spikes,
locked it again,
and disappeared
into the mansion
for another week.

Every Saturday the grown-ups watched.
The boys and girls watched.
Even the dogs watched,
tugging at the ends of their leashes,

wanting to check out
this Charles Larue.

Sometimes folks spoke
to one another
after Charles Larue had passed.
"There is something odd
about that man,"
they said.
And,
"No one who keeps to himself so much
can be trusted."
Whoever heard
"There's something odd
about that man"
or
"No one who keeps to himself so much
can be trusted"
would nod in solemn agreement.

Except the mayor.

The mayor
didn't put up with gossip
any more than she put up with puppies,
and she always said,

"Charles Larue is a citizen
of this town.
He has never caused
a single problem.
He pays the taxes
on that big house
twice a year
and on time.
What more is there
to say?"

The good citizens of Erthly,
and the ornery ones too,
always decided
there was,
indeed,
nothing more to say . . .
at least not
in front of the mayor.

But Charles Larue?
No one knew a single true thing
about him.
They didn't know
what he might long for
beyond bread

and peanut butter,
apples
and baked beans
and a large Milky Way candy bar.
They didn't know
that he had served his lady
with quiet joy
for nearly fifty years.
And they certainly didn't know
that he had once
been in love
with the redheaded waitress
in the Erthly Café,
who'd served him coffee and pie
every week
on his afternoon off.
They didn't know,
because the redheaded waitress
herself
had never known.
Shy Charles Larue had never spoken
his love,
and she'd left Erthly
years before,
convinced
that love must lie

elsewhere.

So Charles Larue had stayed on
in the enormous house
even after his lady was gone.
And the town folks knew as little
about Charles Larue
as they had ever known
about his lady.

So many stories hidden
in even the smallest town.
So many stories
waiting
to be revealed.

8

Buddy barely ate.
She didn't play at all.
The woman didn't seem to know
how to play, anyway . . .
at least not with a dog.
She never threw Buddy's ball.
She didn't pick up
the orange-marmalade stuffed cat

and pretend she was going to run off with it.
She didn't take Buddy's pointy face
between her hands
and kiss her on the lips.

She did feed Buddy.
She let her out into the yard
and picked up what Buddy left there.
And sometimes she patted
the top of Buddy's head
with the flat of her hand,
as though she were bouncing
a ball.
"Good dog," she would say.
"You're a good dog."
But she sounded uncertain,
which made Buddy uncertain too.
Was she still a good dog?

Buddy slept.
She ate some of the kibble the woman put down,
but not very much.
She went out into the backyard
and did what a dog does
on the grass.
And she gazed through the fence,

waiting for her boy
to come back.

Then she slept some more.

Sometimes Buddy woke in the night
feeling so alone
in the world
that she pointed her muzzle
toward the darkness
where the ceiling lived during the day
and howled.

"Quiet, Buddy!"
the woman would call
from behind the door
she closed
when she went to bed.
"Please, be quiet!"
she'd say again
if Buddy didn't obey.
And finally,
if Buddy's cries
went on,
filling the darkness,
the behind-the-door voice

would shout,
"BUDDY,
SHUT UP!"

Buddy
always
shut
up.

But that didn't keep
her heart
from howling.

Mark and his friends
gathered
beneath the enormous old oak
and talked and talked,
their voices clambering
over one another.
Mark had been right.
Everyone loved the idea of a dog park.
And they loved
the idea of a rally
to bring a dog park

to Erthly.

Nearly all the plans
were in place.
Tomorrow evening
they would march
down the middle of Walnut Street,
right to the basement
of the Catholic Church,
where the town council
would be meeting.
The boys,
the girls,
the dogs,
and Fido
too.
Several times during the discussion
Mark had to run a hand
over his bristly brown hair
to keep his courage from flagging.
What would his mother say?
Everything was moving so fast!
But plans had to move fast,
he reminded himself.
So, fast was good.

Wasn't it?

Samantha and Alex
had decided they would paint signs.
Lia was going to make up chants.
Trent and Fido
would lead the parade.
All the dogs
were going to be there,
so,
of course,
Fido was coming too.
(Everyone had agreed
that pets were
citizens of Erthly,
and so they had to be in the rally.
Mark had rubbed his bristly hair
extra hard
over that one.)

"Let's call ourselves
the Dog-Park Pack,"
Alex said.
"The Dog-Park Pack!"
everyone shouted,

and they pumped their fists in the air.
Then they yelled it again
because it sounded so good.
"The Dog-Park Pack!"

The ancient oak
seemed to approve of their plans.
Dog park, it whispered.
The Dog-Park Pack!

But when all of that had been settled,
the most important question
still remained.
"Who'll make a speech
to the town council?"
Mark asked.

Silence.
Everyone looked
off through the iron fence
as though
something very interesting
were happening
behind the blank,
staring
windows

of the mansion.
Then they looked at Mark.
"*You'll* do it!"
Alex
and Samantha
and Ryan
and Lia
and Trent
said in one voice.

"But the mayor is my mother!"
Mark said.
"And she doesn't want to hear
about dog parks
from me."

"She'll have to hear,"
Lia said,
"because she's the mayor,
and the mayor's job
is to listen.
You've always said so."

"But I don't have a dog,"
Mark said.
"I don't even have

a cat who thinks he's a dog!"

"That's all right,"
Samantha told him.
"You'll be speaking for the common good."
(Samantha's mom was a lawyer.
That's why she knew phrases like
"the common good.")

"I've never made a speech before,"
Mark said.

"Nothing to it,"
Ryan told him.
"You just open your mouth
and talk."

"If there's nothing to it,
then why don't you—,"
Mark started to say.
But just then a door opened
in the big house
behind the spiked iron fence,
and Charles Larue
stepped out

onto the broad porch.

Instantly
all Mark's friends decided
it was time
to go home.

"Wait!"
Mark called after them.
But no one waited.
They didn't even
look
back.

Buddy grew sadder and sadder.
She grew thinner and thinner.
When the woman put her bowl of kibble
on the kitchen floor,
Buddy always slid her gaze
toward the bowl,
but she didn't get up
to eat.

Maybe later,
when she walked by,
she'd take a bite
or even two.
But she never ate enough
to fill her belly
or to make her black coat
glossy again.

"I thought dogs were always hungry,"
the woman said.
"That goes to show
how little I know
about dogs."

When Buddy went out
into the yard
to use the grass,
she didn't run back to the door
to be near her new owner.
Instead she settled
into the corner
against the fence
and peered through the slats,
waiting for her boy

to come back.

He didn't,
of course.

We know why he didn't.
We know
her boy wasn't ever going to come walking back
from the faraway city
down the sidewalk
up to the fence
where Buddy waited.

But Buddy knew nothing
of the city
that had swallowed
her boy.
She knew only that there was a place
deep beneath her ribs
that ached
day and night.

11

It wasn't that Charles Larue

had ever done anything
to scare the kids.
It was just
that they had told one another
so many stories about him,
no one could quite remember
what was story
and what was fact.

If you live in a small town like Erthly,
you know most
of the people
there.
But since no one actually knew Charles Larue,
the kids had to make do
with stories.

There were the stories
about ghosts
in Charles Larue's attic,
lost
and lamenting.

There were the stories
about corpses
in Charles Larue's cellar,

unburied
and stinking.

There were even stories
about how he turned into a vampire
whenever the moon
grew fat.
Kids said he skulked across town,
thirsting
for innocent
blood!
(Why is the blood
that vampires thirst for
always said to be innocent?
Wouldn't guilty blood
taste just as good?)

So many stories!
So many kids full of stories!
And here stood Charles Larue
watching
the boys and girls
hurry
away
down the street.
He watched Mark,

too,
standing
alone
beneath the oak tree.

Mark decided it was time
for him to go home
as well.

12

Buddy lay curled
in the corner of the yard,
tight against
the picket fence.
She lay with her pointy nose
tucked
beneath her whiplike tail,
her airplane-wing ears
sagging.

Her entire body
remembered
her boy.
The itch
behind her left ear
remembered his scratching hand.

Her lips
remembered his kiss.
Her legs
remembered leaping
after a high-flung ball.
All gone . . .
gone.
Buddy rose
from the ground.
She turned around
twice,
three times.
She lay down
again.
She got up once more.

Some of the dirt
in the corner,
right close to the fence,
was loose.
Some of the dirt
looked soft,
easy to dig.

Buddy tested it with a paw.
She tested it with both paws.
She threw the dirt behind her,

grandly,
wildly.
She kept on digging.

"Bad dog!"
came a voice from the house.
"Bad, bad dog!
You're ruining
my yard!"

Buddy stopped digging.
She lay down.
She tucked her pointy nose
beneath
her whiplike tail.
She sighed
deeply.

For just a moment there,
she had
almost
been having
fun.

13

Charles Larue stood

in the big double doorway
watching the children
disappear down the street.
They always did that.
Whenever he came outside
to see what they were doing,
they ran away.

He didn't know why they ran.
He had never spoken an unkind word
to a child of Erthly.
In fact,
he'd never spoken any word at all.

He liked children,
certainly.
He'd always wished
he'd had a child
of his own.
He'd been proud
to take care of his lady,
but a child would have been nice.
Maybe two or three.
Perhaps a dog
as well.
But for that to have happened
he'd have needed a different kind of life.

For that to have happened
he'd have needed to find the courage
to say more than
"Pecan pie and coffee, please"
to the redheaded waitress
at the Erthly Café.

In the life he'd been given,
children and dogs
never seemed
to want to come near.

Charles Larue thrust his hands
deep into his pockets
and turned back
to his enormous,
empty
house.

14

For a long time
Buddy lay curled
in the corner
by the fence.
When she stood,

finally,
she turned to examine
the soft dirt
once more.
She patted it.
She poked at it.
She tossed it behind her.
One paw full,

two.
She stopped to study the house.
Nothing.
Not a sign.
Not a sound.
Maybe the woman had gone away.
People had a way of doing that.
Buddy began digging again.

When the hole was deep,
crumbly,
and coolly inviting,
she scooted
under the fence
and out
into the world.
The world where
she was sure
her boy
waited.

Buddy padded a few steps,
then paused
to look back.
She had never been on her own
before.

Behind her,
on the other side of the fence,
she had a bowl,
a bed,
a ball.
(She had chewed up her bone,
and no new one
had appeared.)
Behind her,
on the other side of the fence,
she had an orange-marmalade stuffed cat,
the one she used to toss into the air
and catch again.
The one she still
rested her chin on at night
when she slept.

Buddy's paws hesitated.
Even her paws remembered
the orange-marmalade cat.

But then she thought about her boy,
about chasing balls,
ear scratches,
kisses.
And she set off again

at
a
steady
lope.

15

"Mom,"
Mark said,
"what do people do
when they want to make a speech
to the town council?"
"A speech?" his mother asked.
"Well," Mark said,
"how do people tell the council
when there is something
they want
the town to do?"

"They just come
to the meeting
and talk.
They tell us
what they want."

Mark nodded.
Talking sounded easy.

It was a better word
than "speech."
Except that he hated talking
in front of his class
in school.
What would it feel like
to talk
in front of
the entire
town
council?
In front of his mother, too!

His mother ran her hand
across his bristly brown hair.
"Hey, little porcupine,"
she said,
"why do you want to know
about the town council?"

"Just wondered,"
he said.

Mark turned away,
smiling.
He liked being called
little porcupine.

At least he liked hearing
his mother say it
when no one else was around.
But he knew—
maybe she did too—
that for all their fierce prickles,
porcupines were exceedingly soft
underneath.

Tomorrow he had to talk to the town council.
But could he?

16

Buddy danced
along the sidewalk.
She was looking for her boy's house.
She was looking for
her boy.
I'm coming!
I'm coming!
her faithful heart sang.
I'm here!

She stopped to consider
a tall white house.
But that wasn't it.

She sniffed the bushes
alongside a brick bungalow.
That wasn't it either.
She traveled
through several backyards.
None had the right look,
the right smell.
In fact,
nothing Buddy found
was right.
None belonged
to her boy.

Finally,
more because she was tired—
and a bit discouraged—
than because it seemed like the right one,
she went up onto the porch
of a stucco house
with green shutters
and lay down
in front of the door.
A black Lab
barked
from behind the picture window.

Go away! he barked.

Go!
This house is mine,
mine,

mine,

mine!

Buddy didn't bark back.
She just lay there,
waiting
for whatever
or whoever
was going to happen
next.

17

"What are you doing here?"
The woman opened the door
and flapped a dish towel
at Buddy.
"Shoo!"
she said.
"Go away!"

Buddy leapt to her feet,
but then she stood there.

She didn't know what to do!
In her whole life
no one had ever said
"Shoo!"
to her before.

A man came to the door
too.
"Obviously a stray,"
he said.
"Just see how thin she is."
He opened the door a crack,
but when Buddy looked up at him
hopefully,
he closed it again.
"We should call the dogcatcher,"
he said.
"Except this town is too small
for a dogcatcher.
Do you suppose the sheriff
would have time to come?"

Buddy tipped her head
to one side.
"Dogcatcher"?
"Sheriff"?

She didn't understand those words
either.

"Can we keep her?"
a girl asked,
appearing between the man and the woman.
"Please,
please,
please,
can we keep her?"

"No,"
the man and the woman said together.
"What would we do
with two
dogs?"
the woman said.
She said it
the way grown-ups sometimes do,
as though she were asking a question,
when,
of course,
she didn't want an answer at all.
The little girl answered anyway.
"I'd love them both,"
she said,

reasonably enough.

The door
shut.

Buddy plodded
down the steps
and out to the sidewalk.
The sun had dropped
behind the steeple
of the Catholic Church.
Walnut Street stood empty.
Was there no one who wanted
a little black dog
with brown paws
and a brown mask
and a sweet ruffle of brown fur on her bum
just beneath her black whip of a tail?

No one at all?

18

Charles Larue trudged
through the mansion,
a dust cloth in his hand.

He smoothed the cloth over
this vase,
that figurine,
the cracked feet of the old velvet sofa.

The enormous house echoed
with the *tap-tap-tap* of his feet
on the polished floor,
with their *hush-shush*
on the carpet.
The rocking chair creaked
when he gave it a push.
A small figurine clinked
into place on the shelf.
But Charles Larue paid no attention
to the echoes
in the old house.
Only the dust held him,
the constant,
constant
dust.

He paused at a desk,
opened a drawer
and touched a sheaf of papers.
He didn't need to unfold the papers

to know what they said.
"Last Will and Testament,"
they said.
"The house to Charles Larue,"
they said.
"The house
and the land
and the tall iron fence
with spikes."
He shut the drawer
and sighed.

A dozen times a day
he did that,
opened the drawer,
touched the papers,
shut the drawer,
sighed.

Who knew his lady
would go off
to die among strangers?
No matter
that they called themselves family,
they were strangers.
Who knew she would die

and leave this house,
this enormous old house
and all its dust
to him?

When his lady had lived,
he had promised
he would keep this house,
always.
For her.
Now
if he could wish his promise away,
he would.
He would gladly wish
the whole huge house
away.
What good was an empty house?
What good was
an empty man?

Charles Larue ran his dust cloth
over a picture
on the wall
and sighed again.
His house.
His.

ᕬ

He'd had a good life,
taking care of his lady.
He had prepared her meals.
He'd kept the furnace running
and the lawn neat.
He'd driven her into the countryside
on Sunday afternoons.
He'd been a young man
when he'd come to her,
almost a boy.
She'd called him Larue.
Just that.
"The dinner is lovely, Larue."
"Larue, thank you for driving so carefully."
"What would I do without you, Larue?"

A good life.

Everything he had done
for his lady
he had done
with care and with satisfaction.
But never
in his saddest dreams
had he thought he'd spend

his last years
dusting
this enormous old house
for no one
at all.

Charles Larue moved on
to
the
next
room,
dust cloth in his hand.

19

Buddy trotted along in the gathering dark,
searching.
She passed a school
and three churches,
a grocery store,
a post office,
a hardware store,
a bank.
But she paid no attention
to any of it.
She turned
into the town park

to sniff at the base of a tree.
Dogs she had never met
had left messages there.
She added a comment
of her own,
then settled
beneath the rusty swings.

She laid her chin on her paws.
How she missed
her orange-marmalade stuffed cat!

She thought about going back
to the house
where the woman didn't throw balls
and didn't kiss her
on the lips
and didn't pick up
the stuffed cat
and pretend to run off with it.
But she had left
in such a hurry
that she had quite forgotten
how to go back.

The truth was,
she was lost.

Little dog,
lost.

20

A couple
strolled through the park.
His arm circled her waist.
Her head rested on his shoulder.
Boots crunched.

Sneakers whispered through the grass.

"See that mongrel over there?"
said the boots.
"Must be a stray."

"Dear little dog,"
the sneakers said.
"What's she doing
alone
in the park
at night?
The poor thing must be lost."

"Careful!"
said the boots.
"Don't go close.
You never know
about strays!"

"Who's she going to hurt?"

asked the sneakers.
"See how small she is?"

"You can never be sure,"
the boots said.
And then,
"Hey, you!
Out of here!
Shoo!"

This time Buddy understood
the word.
No problem.
She scrambled
from beneath the swings
and ran.
She didn't pause to look back at the voices,
coaxing and cross,
until she reached the edge of the park.

"Shoo!" the boots said again.
"Go!"

Buddy shooed,
head low,
tail tucked,

airplane ears sagging.

When the park lay far behind,
she stopped beneath
the protective cover
of an old oak tree.
She sat on her ruffled bum.
She tipped her head back
and howled,
long and loud.

21

Mark lay in his pajamas
on top of the bedcovers.
He often lay on top of the bedcovers
on summer nights.
The breeze that slipped
through his window
kept him cool.
And that way
he didn't have to make his bed
in the morning.

A fresh puff of air

stirred his bristly brown hair.

Before he'd gone to bed,
he had spent hours—
at least it had seemed like hours—
trying to write a speech
for the town council.
His wastebasket was full
of failed attempts.
He'd finally come up with two sentences,
the barest kind of start,
just two sentences
worth keeping.
"Dogs need to run and play," he'd written.
"Kids need to run and play with their dogs."
That was hardly enough,
but he hoped,
once he'd said those two sentences,
the rest would come.

He closed his eyes.
Tomorrow evening
he had to speak
in front of the entire town council.
In front of his mother, too.

What would she say when she saw him

and all his friends
and all their dogs
and Fido,
the orange-marmalade cat,
at the council meeting?
Even if she said nothing,
what would her face say?
Would a crease dig deep
into that pale space
between her eyebrows?
Would her eyes spark?
Would her mouth make a straight, tight line?

Would she be angry
or,
even worse,
would she be
disappointed . . .
in him?

Were dogs really citizens of Erthly?

Was Mark
himself
a citizen of Erthly?
Or was he
only

the
mayor's
son?

He'd gone to bed
finally,
but every time he'd fallen asleep,
he'd jerked awake
again,
his heart pounding,
his face hot.
Always it was the same dream.
He stood
in front of his friends
and in front of the town council
and in front of his mother,
his mouth filled with sand.
Not a word would come out.
That wasn't the worst part,
though.
The worst part
was what he was wearing
in his dream.
Or rather
what he wasn't wearing.
He stood in front
of practically the whole town

with nothing on at all!
Naked!
Bare!
And everyone stared at him,
stared and waited for him to speak,
and he had nothing,
nothing,
nothing.
Nothing on
and nothing
to say.
Not even
two sentences.

Now he lay awake
on top of the covers,
waiting for the next puff of breeze
to dry the sweat
of his dream.

He didn't intend to go back to sleep again.
He'd just lie there,
waiting for morning
to come,
waiting for the day
of his humiliation
to come.

22

A cry
drifted along Walnut Street,
more mournful than any tears.
It rode a puff of breeze
into the bedroom
where Mark lay,
holding himself awake.
Bark! Bark! Bark!
A-wooooo-ooo-ooo!
Bark! Bark!
Awooo!

Mark popped up like a jack-in-the-box.

The cry came again,
thin and clear.
It sounded exactly like,
"Mark, Mark, Mark.
I need yoooo-ooo-oou!"

Surely he was imagining things.

Wasn't he?

Still,

he slipped from his bed,
tiptoed into the hall
and through the living room
to the front door.
He moved stealthily,
careful not to bump the small table
where he and his mother
deposited the gatherings
from their day
when they came in.
He turned the door handle . . .
quietly,
quietly.
He stepped outside.
At the edge of the front stoop,
he paused
to listen
again.

The night thrummed
with crickets,
wood frogs,
cicadas.
The poplar tree
in the front yard
rustled its usual
Hush . . . shush . . . shhhh!

Nothing more.

"Call me again," he whispered.
"Please, call me!"

Mark! Mark!
came the response,
as though the owner of the voice
had heard him
and obeyed.
I need yooooooooou!

Mark vaulted down the steps
and set off
toward the voice,
running.

23

Charles Larue stood in the tower
beneath the witch's-hat roof,
looking out over Erthly.

The little town was dark,
just a streetlight

here and there.
The lights weren't bright enough
even to show up
the potholes on Walnut Street
or the rusty swings in the park.
Nor were they bright enough
for Charles Larue to see
the black and brown dog
with airplane ears
sitting beneath the oak tree
by the tall iron fence
with spikes.
His own fence.
His own spikes.

He could hear,
though.
Not the potholes or the rusty swings,
but *Bark, bark, bark.*
A-wooo-ooooo!

One long-ago winter night
he had heard a call like that.
It had been a stray
shivering
at the iron gate.

Charles Larue had asked his lady
what he should do.
"Shall I bring it in?" he'd said.
"The poor thing
must be cold and hungry."
"Do you know anything about dogs,
Larue?"
his lady had asked.
"No," he'd had to admit.
"I've never had a dog
in my life."
"Can you tell if this one is sick?
Or full of fleas?"
"Probably not,"
he'd said.
"Then, I think we'd better take
the creature
to someone who knows more
about dogs
than we do,"
she had replied,
not unkindly.
And he had put the dog in the car
and taken it
to an animal shelter.
in the next town.

When he'd come back,
he had cleaned the car
very thoroughly.
What,
after all,
did he know about dogs,
sick or well,
flea-ridden or not?

And that was the last time
he had been near
a dog.

Bark, bark, bark.

He knew no more about dogs now
than he had then.
He certainly wouldn't know
what to do with one
if he took it in.

A-wooooooooo!

Nonetheless,
Charles Larue
hurried down

the winding stairs
toward the sound.

24

A block from his house,
Mark stopped
in the middle
of Walnut Street,
remembering.
His mother had rules,
important rules.
Erthly was a small town,
a safe town.
But even in a small, safe town
you didn't leave your bed
in the middle of the night
and,
without telling a soul,
hurry down the main street
in your pajamas,
in your bare feet.
Not even when you heard
your name
being called

by a dog.

What if his mother woke
and found
him missing?

For a long moment
Mark stood
still
in the silence.
"Call me again,"
he whispered.
If he heard nothing more,
he would go back
to his bed.
He would go back
to lying awake
in his bed.

And then
there it was!
Yooo-oo-u!

Mark's heart lurched.
It seemed to be trying

to free itself
from the cage of his ribs
to reach the voice
even
before
he
got
there.

He followed
his pounding heart
toward the sound.

25

Charles Larue threw open the big double doors
with the lion's-head knockers,
hurried across the broad porch
and down the walk,
unlocked the gate
in the tall iron fence,
and pushed through
to the other side.

And there,
there,

beneath the oak tree . . .
a dog.
A small dog
with the funniest-looking ears
he had ever seen.

And there
too . . .
a boy,
running fast toward the dog!

Charles Larue stood
perfectly still,
waiting to see
what
would
happen
next.

26

Just as Mark approached the oak tree
in the night dark,
he saw the gate open.
He could make out a small man
with a great bush of white eyebrows

and a great beak of a nose.
(There wasn't enough light
to make out
the robin's-egg blue
of the eyes
between eyebrows
and nose.)

In the night dark
he could also make out a small dog
with airplane ears
that drooped
just at the tips.
Such sweet ears!

Mark knew the man,
of course.
It was the mysterious Charles Larue.
Mark didn't know the dog,
but
certainly
this was the one
that had been calling him.

Seeing Charles Larue
stopped

Mark's feet
cold.
Seeing Buddy started them up again . . .
slowly,
cautiously.

"Here, little dog," he called.
"Come, dog."
Mark kept his gaze
on Charles Larue
as he spoke.
He didn't really believe all those stories.
At least he didn't think he did.
Still,
though his hand,
stretching toward the dog,
held steady,
his voice wavered
just a bit.

"Here, little dog."

Charles Larue watched the boy,
watched the dog.
Both boy and dog
were coiled springs,

waiting to be released.
What were they doing here
outside his gate
in the night,
anyway?

Buddy stretched toward the reaching hand.
She touched it,
just lightly
with her cool, damp nose.
A boy hand.
A good boy hand.
She breathed it in.

And Mark,
feeling the coolness,
the dampness
of the nose
and the snuffle of warm breath
against his palm,
fell instantly,
deeply,
helplessly
in love.
This . . .
this . . .

this little dog
was exactly what he'd begged for,
what he'd longed for,
what he'd needed
his entire life!

If only his mother . . .
But no,
there was no point
in expecting his mother
to change.
He'd been asking for a dog
forever,
and the answer
had always been the same.
Besides,
how could he expect his mother—
his practical,
no-nonsense mother—
to believe
that a stray dog
had called his name
in the night?

Mark took a step forward
anyway.

Close enough
to reach down and gather the dog
into his arms . . .
if she would let him.
What he would do with her
after he picked her up,
he had no idea.
But he needed to hold her,
if only for a few seconds.

That step,
though—
that one step—
was too much
for Buddy.
Instead of remembering
all the good boy moments
that had filled her life,
she remembered, "Shoo!"
She remembered, "Go away!"
She remembered flapping dish towels
and cross voices.
The spring that held her tight
sprung.
Without even deciding,
she found herself running
fast,

fast,
fast.

But where she was going,
she had no idea.

Away.
Only that.

Away.

27

Mark stood
with his hand still out,
facing the great bush of white eyebrows
and the great beak of a nose.
The night was too dark
to make out the eyes
between eyebrows and nose,
but he imagined them fierce.
He imagined them cruel.
And in that sudden imagining
Mark remembered
what he had almost forgotten.

His mother.

If she woke
and found him gone,
she would be wild with worry.
If she woke
and found him gone,
she would be furious!
She wouldn't be much interested
in hearing why he'd gone out
wandering the streets
of Erthly
in the middle of the night.
She would know,
with great certainty,
that he never should have left
his bed.

Mark took a long look
at the little dog
disappearing down the street,
then at the silent man
standing
before him.

He turned
and ran
toward

home.

28

Little dog running.
Little dog scurrying,
scampering,
panting.
Nowhere to go.
No one to take her in.

Little black dog with brown paws
and a brown mask
and a sweet ruffle of brown fur on her bum
just beneath the black whip of her tail.

Little dog,
lost,
lost,
lost.

29

Charles Larue stood
for a long time
in front of his own iron gate,

the one with spikes.

The boy was gone.

The dog was gone.

Why hadn't he spoken?

His voice had grown rusty
with disuse,
but surely he still knew how
to speak.

What would he have said,
though?
What did he have left to say?

A breeze stirred the oak tree
above his head,
setting the leaves murmuring
to one another.
Sssspeak . . . sssspeak,
they seemed to say.
Charles Larue sighed.
Even an old oak tree
had more to say

to the world
than he did.

He turned and plodded back
toward
the huge,
empty
house.

30

This is,
perhaps,
the moment to pause
to consider
longing.
Mark's longing for a dog.
Buddy's longing for a boy.
Charles Larue's longing for something . . .
boy or dog or his lost lady,
anything to give his life shape again.

Mark went back to his bed,
carefully stepping around
the small, cluttered table
just inside the door,

still longing.
Buddy ran through town,
searching for a place
to hide,
still longing.
Charles Larue listened to the echo
of the large double doors
closing behind him,
then stood
in the foyer
longing for . . .
he didn't know what.
But there was no question;
he was longing too.

And let us not forget the first boy,
now living in the city,
the one who'd
given
Buddy
up.

He woke that same night
and gazed at the many-colored lights
that streamed through his window.
All night long in the city,
light streamed.

Not many dogs in the city,
but lots of light.

The boy liked the lights.
Sometimes he climbed out of bed
and sat
at his bedroom window,
to watch the colors
dance up and down
the always-busy street.

He'd found a friend yesterday.
His first one in the city.
His friend didn't have a dog
either,
but he'd liked hearing
about Buddy.
The boy had told his new friend
everything:
about her fantastic ears,
about how high she could leap
to catch a ball,
about the stuffed cat
she rested her chin on when she slept.
He hadn't mentioned
the kisses,
though.

Somehow
he hadn't wanted
to talk
about the kisses.
Still . . .
he'd told his new friend about his dog,
and he hadn't cried.
It was the first time
he'd managed to talk about Buddy
without crying.

That didn't change the promise
he had made to himself,
though,
the promise he'd made every single day
since the move.
When he was grown,
he would have a dog again,
and, big or small,
rough-coated or smooth,
male or female,
his dog would be named Buddy.

And the boy,
who would then be a man,
would never
give Buddy

away.

Ever.

So much longing.
So many lives
filled
with longing.

It's what stories—
all our stories—
are made of.

And what is longing
made of
except hope?

31

Sunlight danced across the kitchen table.
It glinted in Mark's orange juice
and skittered across his bowl of cereal.

"What are you going to do today?"
his mother asked.

Mark knew

exactly
what he was going to do.
He was going to search for the little dog
he had found
last night.
But he didn't say that.

"Just ride my bike,
I guess," he said.
It was the truth,
after all.
That was exactly what he was going to do,
ride his bike
all over town,
searching.
"I'll probably see some of my friends,"
he added,
"and their *dogs*."
The word "dogs"
came out as hard as a stone,
but his mother
didn't seem to notice.

"I'm working until five,"
she said.
Mark nodded.

He didn't need to be told that.
His mother worked at the post office,
and she usually stayed until five.
(In a small town like Erthly,
being mayor
wasn't a job.
It was more like being
an elected volunteer.)
"I have a council meeting
at seven tonight,"
she said.
Mark knew that, too.
He was going to be there.
"So supper will be early."
Mark nodded again.

Mark's mother gave his bristly hair
a gentle tug,
as though he might not be
paying attention,
though he had heard
every word.
"Check in
with Mrs. Morgan
before you go anywhere,"
she said.

"Let her know where you'll be."

Mark didn't need to be told that,
either.
He *always* checked in
with Mrs. Morgan.
She lived next door,
and she'd looked after him
while his mother worked
since he was a baby.
Besides,
Mrs. Morgan always kept
a plate of freshly baked cookies
on her kitchen table.
Her snickerdoodles
were famous.

"And Mark?"
his mother said.
He looked up,
saw the crease
between her eyebrows,
and looked away.
"I heard a dog howling last night,"
she said.

"It was carrying on something awful.
Must be a stray.
I'll let the sheriff know.
He'll take care of it.
In the meantime
I want you to be careful.
Don't go near
any stray dogs.
You never know."

Mark tried on a smile,
though it didn't fit very well.
You never know,
he thought,
when a stray dog
might be calling your name.

Then he gave his mom a hug,
stopped by to check in
with Mrs. Morgan
(and collect a snickerdoodle),
and rode off
on his bike.

He had a mission now

for certain.
He had to save
a lost dog
from the sheriff.

"Here, dog!" he called,
again and again.
"Here, little dog."

But no little dog
with airplane ears
appeared.

32

Buddy stood in the alley
behind the house.
There it was.
At last.
She'd found it.
But even though she knew
this was the house
she'd come from,
she didn't move.

Her bed was there.

Her ball,
her bowl,
her kibble,
all were there.
Buddy's stomach rumbled
when she thought
about her kibble.

Her cat was there too,
her orange-marmalade stuffed cat.

But the woman was in that house too.
The one who yelled,
"Shut up, Buddy."
The one who said,
"No!"
The one who patted her head
with a stiff,
flat hand
and said, "Good dog,"
but didn't seem to mean it.

Buddy checked the fence.
The hole she had dug
had been filled in.
She tested the dirt.

Soft,
loose.
She could dig it again.
She could dig it
and crawl back inside
as easily as she had crawled out.

But she didn't.

Instead
she turned,
head hanging,
ears hanging,
tail hanging,
and walked
away.

She had a boy.
She knew she had a boy.
Somewhere.

33

Mark rode his bike along Walnut Street.
He was getting good
at hitting all the potholes.

He turned up First Avenue,
along Maple Street,
across Second Avenue,
down Birch Street.
"Here, dog," he called
the length of every street.
"Here, little dog.
Come to me!
Please!"

If he had known to peek
beneath the porch
of the brick house
on the corner of Walnut and Fifth,
he would have found Buddy,
lying in the cool dark.
But he didn't know.

"Here, dog.
Come, little dog."

Buddy heard.
She lifted her head.
She thumped
her whiplike tail.
She strained

her airplane ears
to capture the boy voice,
the good boy voice.

"Come to me.
Please?"

But it wasn't *her* boy voice.

She lowered her head.
Her airplane ears
drooped.
Her tail went still.

In the hidden dark beneath the porch
Buddy closed her eyes
and slept
again.

Mark rode on,
calling.
"Here, dog!
Come, little dog.
Come to me.
Please?"

No little dog came.

34

The summer evening
lay across Erthly
like a wool blanket,
heavy and smothering,
without a breath of breeze.
Thunder stammered in the distance.
Storm coming.
Storm coming,
it warned.
But the Dog-Park Pack
had more important things
to think about
than a little rain.

They had gathered
once more
beneath the enormous oak tree
next to the iron fence
with spikes,
ready to do battle
with the town council.

Cinder,
the schnoodle,
danced around Ryan's feet,

tangling his legs.
Blizzard,
the white shepherd,
sat next to Alex,
as stately as a statue.
Hotdog,
the dachshund,
found something wonderfully smelly
in the grass
and rolled in it.
Fido,
the orange-marmalade cat,
touched noses
with each of his dog friends,
then sat down primly
at the end of his leash
and washed his right paw.
When he was done
he used the slick of spit
on his paw
to clean his magnificent whiskers.
He cleaned them
with the kind of care
that made it clear
he knew
exactly

how magnificent
they were.

Lia arrived with Polly and Daisy,
her aunt's goldens.
Daisy pranced over to check out Hotdog.
Then,
pleased with Hotdog's new smell,
she rolled in the grass too.
(The wonderful scent
in the grass
had been left,
quite recently,
by a passing rabbit.)

Samantha handed out signs on sticks.
The signs said
A KID'S BEST FRIEND
and
EQUAL PLAY FOR CANINES
and
DOGS ARE CITIZENS TOO.

"You don't say anything about dog parks,"
Mark said.
"I don't need to,"

Samantha replied.
"You're going to talk about dog parks."

Mark nodded.
Of course.
He was going to talk about dog parks.
In front of the town council.
In front of his mother.
He had said he would,
so he would,
though he still wasn't sure
what would come tumbling out
after
his two
opening
sentences.

"My sign talks about dog parks."
Alex held up a huge sign that said
DOG PARKS FOR DOGS!
FREEDOM FROM LEASHES!

"Dog parks for dogs!"
Lia chanted.
"Freedom from leashes!"
Everyone joined in,

"DOG PARKS FOR DOGS!
FREEDOM FROM LEASHES!"
The Dog-Park Pack was as loud
as the sign was big.

Mark thought about Charles Larue
standing
right here
beneath the oak tree
last night.
Mark looked over his shoulder
toward the iron gate,
where the man had appeared.
Nothing.
Still, a chill traveled along his spine,
and his gaze skittered
to the tower.
Was a shadow lurking there,
leaning
close
to the window?

"Let's go,"
he said to his friends,
and he ushered everyone
ahead of him

down the street.
Not that he was in a hurry
to get there.
He was only in a hurry
to leave.

Trent and Fido led the parade.
The rest followed.
"THE DOG-PARK PACK!"
everyone shouted.
Once more

they pumped their fists
in the air.

Thunder muttered and growled.
The storm
moved
closer.

35

When the parade went by
the corner of Fifth Avenue
and Walnut Street,
Buddy woke.
Her head popped up.
Her airplane ears flared,
gathering in the sound
of all those dogs,
all those boys and girls.

She tipped her head
to listen more closely.
Then she rose,
gave herself a shake,
and crawled out
from beneath the porch.

Maybe her boy would be there,
in all that good commotion.

She trotted off,
following
the parade.

36

Another drumroll of thunder
announced the Dog-Park Pack
as they marched
down the stairs
and into the basement
of the Catholic Church,
where the town council met.
When they entered the room,
the entire council looked up,
startled.

The mayor looked up,
startled
too.

The Dog-Park Pack
kept marching.
They had work to do,
important work.
Trent,
leading the parade with Fido,
circled the room.
Everyone else followed
until dogs
and boys
and girls
(and Fido, of course)
surrounded
the town council
and the mayor.

The mayor narrowed her eyes,
looking hard at the signs.
A crease dug
into the pale space
between her eyebrows.
Then she looked

at her son.
"Mark?" she said.

Thunder rumbled again,
louder,
closer.
Mark stepped forward.
He looked at each member
of the town council,
and then he looked at the mayor,
his mother.
He squared his shoulders.
He lifted his chin.
He opened his mouth.

No words came out.
It was like his dream.
His mouth seemed to be stuffed
with sand.
In fact,
he had to look down
to make sure
he wasn't standing there
naked.

Thunder again.

Closer.
Louder still.
A blam.
A roar.
A rattling explosion.
Mark's hair stood up
even more stiffly
than usual.

He opened his mouth
once more
He was going to say it:
"Dogs need to run and play.
Kids need to run and play with their dogs."
But before the words
could find their way
to his tongue,
something else happened.
And the something else that happened
was Buddy.

The small black and brown dog,
following the parade,
following the girls
and boys
and dogs

and the tantalizing orange-marmalade cat,
pranced down the stairs
and into the church basement,
where the mayor
and the town council
and the boys
and girls
and dogs . . .
and Fido
waited.
She held her head high.
She held her tail high.
Her eyes sparked,
and she lifted each paw
as though she were performing
a dance
before an admiring crowd.
She didn't look
a bit
like a lost little dog.
She looked like a dog
in pursuit of a dream.

And to everyone's amazement—
and to the horror

of those who knew Fido—
Buddy pranced across the floor
and right up
to the orange-marmalade cat.

Perhaps Buddy was thinking
of her own cat,
the stuffed one she tossed
into the air
and caught again,
the one she liked to lay her chin on
at night
when she slept.
Who knows
what the little dog might have been thinking?
Maybe she didn't even know
that her toy
was a cat.
It might have been only Fido's color
that drew her.
Or it could be that Fido,
who was,
after all,
a very in-charge-of-the-world cat,
had simply commanded her

to come close.

We will never know.

What we can know,
what you already know,
is that Fido couldn't abide dogs
who hadn't learned proper respect.
He had taught all his dog friends
how to approach him . . .
head down,
eyes down,
ears down,
tail down.
And here came this stranger,
ears flying like airplane wings.
Here came this stranger
without a shred of respect
for a living,
breathing,
in-charge-of-the-world—
at least the world of Erthly—
orange-marmalade
cat.

Fido arched his back.

He lowered his head.
His fur spiked all along his spine.
His tail stiffened like a bottle brush.
And he opened his pink mouth
with its pointy teeth
and said, *Shaaaaaah!*
right in Buddy's face.

Buddy went still,
astonished
at the rude greeting.
But even more astonishment
awaited
the little dog.
Because Fido reached out
with a curved claw
and slashed Buddy's tender nose,
right down the middle.

What did Buddy do?
Exactly what you would do
if a claw suddenly tried
to turn your one precious nose
into two.
She yelped.
She squealed.

She hollered.
And she bolted from the room,
her whiplike tail
tucked against her belly.
(I know that,
if it were you,
you'd have no tail to tuck,
but you get the picture.)
Buddy ran so fast,
in fact,
her tail glued
so tightly against her belly,
that you couldn't even see
the sweet ruffle of brown fur
on her bum.

Fido,
however,
wasn't finished
with the conversation.

In one mighty spring
he tugged the leash from Trent's hand
and followed.

Thunder blammed again,

so loudly this time
that even the basement
of the Catholic Church
shook.

37

The room tumbled
with boys
and girls
and dogs.
"Look out!"
"Where'd he go?"
It scattered
with members of the town council.
"Wait!"
"Stop!"
It erupted
with the mayor.
"What is the meaning—"
But even though she was the mayor,
no one answered,
because no one knew
the meaning of anything
at that moment.
Especially not Mark.

He,
like all the rest
of the Dog-Park Pack
and their dogs
and the entire town council,
was too busy bolting up the stairs,
rushing onto the street,
following Fido.

What could the mayor do
but follow too?

And Buddy,
the lost little dog,
ran,
ran,
ran
down the street,
away from furious Fido,
who
ran,
ran,
ran
too!

38

So here's where this story has brought us:
The mayor
and the town council
were tearing down Walnut Street,
chasing the Dog-Park Pack.
The Dog-Park Pack was chasing Fido.
Fido was chasing Buddy.
(Buddy was clearly in the lead,
though where she was heading—
except for away from Fido—
no one knew,
probably not even Buddy herself.)

If you don't mind,
however—
perhaps even if you do—
I'm going to pause this interesting scene
for a moment
to fill you in
on another part of the story.

While this great chase was going on,
something else was happening.

Do you remember the shadow
Mark had glimpsed
at the tower window,
the glimpse that had sent him scurrying
on his mission?
That was,
of course,
Charles Larue,
standing in the tower,
watching,
the way he watched every lonely evening
over Erthly.
This particular evening
he had found the watching
more interesting than usual.
He'd seen a parade with signs,
boys,
girls,
dogs,
and an orange-marmalade cat.
He'd even seen a little dog
with wide-flung ears
crawl out
from beneath the porch
of the brick house
on Walnut Street and Fifth Avenue
and trot along

after
the
parade.

Meanwhile,
when everyone had disappeared
in the direction
of the Catholic Church,
Charles Larue continued to stand,
gazing
out of the tower window.

And the storm
continued to roil into town.

The water tower
at the edge of town
captured a zig of lightning
and sent it plunging
into the ground,
where it could do
no harm.

Another blast
zapped the swing set
in the park.
The bolt sizzled

down the metal chains
and melted the rusty swings
into lumps.
(Don't worry about the swings.
Insurance would soon replace them
with bright new ones
without a speck
of rust.)

Then,
a few moments later,
a final bolt assaulted the tower
where Charles Larue stood,
setting the witch's-hat roof
glimmering.
That was the strike
that made even the basement
of the Catholic Church
tremble.
Flashes of blue,
white,
red,
orange,
a touch of green,
danced

over Charles Larue's head.

For an instant he stood,
transfixed
by the colors.
Then he jolted,
as if from a dream,
and ran
down
the winding
stairs,
through the double doors,
across the wide porch,
along the walk,
and through the gate
in the iron fence,
the one with spikes.
(He had to unlock it,
of course,
but,
fortunately,
he always carried the key
in his pocket.)
He stood in the middle of Walnut Street
and cried,
"Fire! Fire!"

෨

And indeed,
behind him
the peak of the witch's-hat roof
had bloomed into flame
like a birthday candle
on a giant cake
touched
by a giant match.

"Help! Fire!"
Charles Larue shouted again,
and he reached out his arms
as though to some saving force.

To his own surprise . . .
the force came!

Perhaps it wasn't a saving force.
Perhaps it was a force looking to be saved.
But suddenly Buddy,
who—
I know you'll remember—
was dashing down the street
trying with all her might
to stay ahead

of furious Fido,
clambered up Charles Larue's legs,
scrabbled into his arms,
and gave his great beaked nose
a grateful lick.

All the town,
it seemed,
dogs
and cat
and boys
and girls
and council
and mayor
came after.

39

Can you imagine
how amazed Charles Larue was
to find a dog
tucked inside his arm?
But though he had never owned one,
he found that he knew
exactly what to do.
He cradled

the trembling Buddy
against his chest
in a gentle but firm embrace.
And if Buddy was amazed
to discover that she had climbed a man,
she knew what to do too.
She tucked her sore nose
beneath the stranger's chin
and closed her eyes
as tightly as any little dog could.
Perhaps she thought that
If she couldn't see Fido,
he couldn't see her,
either.

But Fido *could* see her.
His eyes were narrowed
to golden slits,
but he could see very well.
And he was still running,
fast.
When he arrived
at the feet of the man
who had rescued Buddy,
he did the same thing Buddy had done
a moment earlier.

He kept right on going.
And the only place to go was up
into Charles Larue's other arm,
directly across from Buddy.

Fido glowered at Buddy.
He lowered his head.
He flattened his ears.
He twitched his tail.
He growled deep in his throat.
And he unsheathed his claws,
ready
for another encounter
with Buddy's nose.

Buddy
just squinched her eyes even tighter
and tried
to disappear
beneath that sheltering chin.

So here we are:
flame sprouting
from the witch's-hat roof
on the tower
of the mansion.

The mayor
and the town council
and the Dog-Park Pack
all running up Walnut Street
toward Charles Larue.
And Charles Larue standing
with Buddy in one arm
and a furious Fido
in the other.
Can you guess what's going to happen next?

More slashing?
More yelping?
Some of the yelping
coming from poor Charles Larue?
That is,
indeed,
Fido's plan,
if a cat could be said to have a plan.

But there is another plan going here,
the story's own plan.
And in aid of that,
something more has been set
into motion,
something besides Fido and his fury.

What's that, you say?
Why,
the racketing storm,
of course.
Until this moment
thunder and lightning
had been banging through Erthly
without a whisper of rain.
Now,
at last,
the rain came in a rush.
It was as though a giant hand
Had pulled a plug on a cloud,
perhaps the same giant hand
that had lit the candle
on Charles Larue's
birthday-cake house.
Rain streamed from the sky,
and in its plunge
it accomplished two things
at once.
It doused
the tongue of flame
licking Charles Larue's tower roof,
as neatly as a puff of birthday breath
puts out a candle.

And it soaked
one very cross cat.

Now, Fido,
as you know,
was already in a bad temper.
From the instant he had seen Buddy
dancing into the basement
of the Catholic Church
as though she had as much right
to be there
as anyone else,
he had been enraged.
A strange dog?
In his town?
One who had never asked
his permission to exist?
And waltzing right up to him that way?
What impudence!
What audacity!
What gall!
He knew how to teach her a lesson!
And he was ready to do
just that.

There was,

however,
one thing Fido hated
even more than an insolent dog.
That was getting wet.
Even a little bit of water—
dew in the grass,
a skim of puddle on the sidewalk,
a misty day—
was an affront
to his paws
and his whiskers
and his fine orange-marmalade fur.
A downpour like this
that soaked him to the skin
in the first breathless torrent
was more than an affront.
It was an outrage!
It was even more of an outrage,
in fact,
than an upstart dog
who needed
to be taught
respect.

And so Fido leapt from Charles Larue's arm
and dashed

for the driest place he knew . . .
home.

Buddy
stayed snugged up close
to the man who had rescued her.
She began licking rain—
and were those tears?—
from Charles Larue's face,
steadily,
thoroughly,
hopefully.

And Charles Larue was,
indeed,
weeping.
He stood
holding the little dog,
surrounded by the mayor
and the town council
and the Dog-Park Pack,
with tears,
as abundant as the rain,
streaming down his face.
The birthday-candle flame
was out.

His beloved house
was saved!
And these good folks
had come when he had called.
Every one of them!
In all his life
nothing so fine had ever happened.
No wonder
he wept.

40

As suddenly as the rain had begun,
it stopped,
and a watery hush fell over Erthly.
No one seemed to notice,
though.
The mayor,
the town council,
the boys
and girls
and dogs
were all too intent
on Charles Larue
to notice how wet they were.

Everyone moved in close.
There is nothing like tears,
you see,
to take the scary out of a man.
An armful of dog
can do it too.
Or a smile like the one that stretched
across Charles Larue's face,
just above Buddy's airplane ears,
almost as wide
as those ears.

With the downpour over,
folks all up and down Walnut Street
emerged from their houses.
They streamed toward the crowd
surrounding Charles Larue.
They didn't know
what the commotion was about,
but whatever it was
looked more interesting
than anything that had happened
in Erthly
for a long time.
A woman with salt-and-pepper hair

came too.

Mark pushed closer
to get a good look at the little dog
in Charles Larue's arms,
the one who kept licking
his face
and his great beaked nose.

Was it?
Could it be?
Yes!
This was the dog he'd been searching for,
the one
he was certain
had called his name
in the night.

Carefully,
he stepped up
to Charles Larue
and presented his palm
to the little dog.
She sniffed it
as she had the night before.
Her nose was still cool and damp,

her breath still warm.
"It's you," Mark said.
"I've been looking for you everywhere."
And Buddy's snuffling breath seemed to say,
also,
It's you! It's you! It's you!

Mark looked at the man
who stood smiling and weeping
with the little dog
tucked in his arm.
"May I hold her?"
he whispered.
"Please?"

Charles Larue peered over the wide-flung ears
at the boy
standing before him,
his spiky brown hair flattened
by its recent soaking.
He didn't especially want to give up
the warm, wet weight of dog
in his arms.
But there was something
about the boy
that tugged at him,

something sweet and sad
that shone in his young face.
"She seems like a fine dog,"
Charles Larue said,
"but, then,
you look like a fine boy."
And he handed Buddy over.

His lady had been right,
after all.
He knew nothing
about dogs.

Mark received Buddy
as he might have taken possession
of a precious chalice,
reverently,
carefully.
He studied her pointy face,
her brown mask,
her airplane ears.
He scratched her
behind one ear,
then the other.
When he got to the left ear,
she leaned into the scratch

and rumbled,
deep in her throat.
Joy bubbled in Mark's chest,
joy and the deepest,
most radiant
desire.
He *wanted* this small black and brown dog.
And he knew,
without a doubt,
that she wanted him,
too.

But when he looked up,
he saw his friends
and all their dogs,
waiting . . .
for him.
They wanted something too.
They wanted a dog park.
And he had made a promise.

As you know,
for all his effort the night before,
Mark hadn't gotten beyond
the first two sentences of his speech.
Any speech

he might have written
wasn't going to do him much good now
anyway.
The town council was here,
but this could hardly be called
a meeting.
Still . . .
he had to say
something.

As Mark searched
for words,
his gaze fell
on the tall iron fence
and on the expanse of green lawn
beyond.
And then his gaze fell
on Charles Larue.
Until just now,
asking to hold the little dog,
Mark had never spoken
to the man
in his life.
He didn't know anyone who had,
except,
perhaps,

his mother,
who spoke to everyone.
And yet . . .
and yet . . .
Charles Larue's eyes seemed so
kind.
And besides being kind,
they seemed sad.

Mark began to speak.
"Dogs need to run and play,"
he said.
"Kids need to run and play
with their dogs."

The crowd grew silent,
listening.

Charles Larue listened
too.
He listened and waited.
And so Mark kept talking,
the idea gathering
even as he spoke.

"I thought,"

he said.
"I mean,
I was wondering if . . ."
He turned and gazed once more
through the iron fence
at the expanse of grass
and the towering trees
surrounding the old mansion.
There was a grove of pine,
a clump of white-barked birch,
a willow
bending gracefully over
a small, shimmering pool.
Mark had never noticed
how beautiful the mansion grounds were.
He had never noticed
what a perfect place they would make
for a dog park.

He looked at Charles Larue
again
and drew in a deep breath.

"Do you like kids?"
he asked.

Charles Larue seemed surprised
by the question,
but he nodded.
His head jerked up and down
as though he
weren't quite accustomed
to saying yes,
but it was definitely a nod.
"What about dogs?"
Mark asked.

Another nod,
this time
smoother.

"And cats?"
Mark added.

Charles Larue hesitated,
for just an instant.
Perhaps he was considering the scratches
up his leg and along his arm
left by the last cat
he had encountered.
But even if he was,
he nodded again

anyway.
"Cats, too,"
he said.
"I've never had kids or dogs or cats
in my life,
but I like them all,
immensely."
And though it was hard to imagine
that such a thing was possible,
his smile grew even wider.

Mark felt an answering smile
softening his own eyes,
tipping his lips,
opening his heart.
And now the words tumbled out
in a rush.
"You could have lots of dogs,"
he said.
"You could have
dogs
and kids.
You could even have a cat
who *thinks* he's a dog.
And you could have them

every single day."
He looked squarely
into Charles Larue's eyes,
and now he could see.
They were as blue as the morning glories
his mother grew
outside her kitchen window.
"Just unlock your gate,"
he said,
"so we could come in.
Your yard
would make
a perfect dog park."

And then he waited,
his breath buried in his chest
like some forgotten
treasure.
The Dog-Park Pack
waited
too.
The town council
waited.
Even the mayor
waited

to see what Charles Larue
would say.

At first the man
said nothing at all.
He merely stared.
He opened his mouth
and then closed it again.
He tried again.
"Unlock the gate so you could visit?"
Surprise sent his voice high,
as though he had never once thought
that anyone
might want to visit
him.
And he hadn't.
"Unlock the gate for a dog park?"
he said.
His smile trembled
at the edges.
His eyes,
between his great bushy white eyebrows
and his great beaked nose,
shone
as crystal blue
as any tears.

"Why," he said,
"nothing would please me more."
And he reached into his pocket
and drew out an iron key.
"I'd love to invite
the children
and the dogs
and even the orange-marmalade cats
of Erthly
to visit
anytime they like."
He looked at each of the Dog-Park Pack
in turn.
He looked at each of the dogs,
too.
He couldn't look at Fido,
because Fido was home
licking his fur dry,
but he remembered Fido
very well.
"Together,"
he said,
"we can make a fine
dog park."

Then

Charles Larue did something
no one
in Erthly
had ever seen him do
before.
He tipped back his head
and laughed.

The mayor,
and the town council,
and the citizens
who had come out of their houses,
and the Dog-Park Pack
laughed
too.

And if dogs could laugh,
I'm sure they would have.
Certainly
they all smiled.

"Yay for Mr. Larue!"
the kids shouted.
"Yay for the Dog-Park Pack!
Yay for the dog park!"

41

Only one person
wasn't laughing,
cheering,
smiling.
The one person
you would have expected
to be the happiest of all.
The one who had come up with the idea
of a dog park
and who had just given a speech
that had brought that dog park to Erthly.

Mark,
of course.

He stood as still as stone.

In the midst of all the commotion,
he had heard
a single voice
that had stopped his rejoicing . . .
and his heart.
"Buddy!"
the voice had called.

"Is that you, Buddy?"

Who was Buddy?

And yet he knew.

Mark squeezed the little dog
so hard that she grunted.
Ooooooomph!
Then he did the only thing
left for him to do.
He waited.

A woman with salt-and-pepper hair
emerged from the crowd,
still talking.
"Buddy,"
she said.
"What a bad dog you are.
I was so worried.
I've been looking everywhere for you.
How could you run away
like that?"

Mark knew the woman.

In fact,
he knew her
well.
Her name was Miss Klein,
and she'd been his first-grade teacher.
Mark had always liked Miss Klein,
but he didn't like her now.

Buddy,
if that was her name—
what a silly name for a girl dog!—
didn't seem to like her
either.
Certainly she didn't try to leap
from Mark's arms
to say hello.
She wagged her tail politely,
just at the tip,
and gave Miss Klein
a limp-eared look.
Then she tucked her sore nose
back beneath Mark's chin.

"Is this your dog, Miss Klein?"
Mark asked.

His voice had gone hoarse.

"*My* dog?"
Miss Klein seemed surprised
at the idea.
"I don't quite think of her as mine,
but I suppose she is.
Friends left her with me
when they moved to the city."
She gave Buddy a considering look.
"I don't think she's very happy
at my house, though,"
she said.
"She dug under the fence
and ran away."
Miss Klein turned up her hands.
I tried,
her hands seemed to say.
I really did.
Then she added,
"I'm afraid I know very little
about dogs."

"I know about dogs,"
Mark said softly.
"I know lots

about dogs."

A long silence followed.
Mark looked at Miss Klein,
and Miss Klein looked at Mark.
At last Miss Klein said,
"Buddy seems happy with you, Mark."
And as if to prove that was so,
Buddy gave Mark's face
a slurpy lick
from his chin
all the way to his left eyebrow.

"I wonder if—,"
Miss Klein started to say,
but just as Mark's heart
began a hopeful patter,
someone stepped out of the crowd.
His mother.
The mayor.

"Hello, Karen,"
she said.

Mark kept his gaze
fastened on Miss Klein's face.

"I wonder if *what?*"
he wanted to cry.
But his mother was standing there,
so he didn't.

Miss Klein smiled at the mayor.
"Hello, Patricia,"
she said.

"I'm glad you've found your dog,"
Mark's mother said.

Miss Klein nodded.
"The truth is,"
she said,
"I don't seem to be doing very well
by *my* dog.
In fact,
the real truth is
I'd be glad if she could find
a better home."

Every muscle
in Mark's body
went still.
Even his heart seemed

to quit beating.
"Mom?"
he said,
his voice trembling.

But his mother went right on talking
to Miss Klein
as though he hadn't spoken.
"Perhaps,"
she said,
"you could put up a notice
on the bulletin board
at the grocery store.
There must be someone
here in Erthly
who wants
a dog."

Someone?
Someone!
Anger zigged through Mark's veins
like lightning.
Didn't his mother see him,
standing here
right in front of her?
Had she never seen him

in his entire life?

"You're right."
Miss Klein said.
"That's what I should do.
I'll post a notice
at the grocery store.
She's a nice dog,
really.
Someone will be happy
to have her."
And as she spoke,
she reached to take Buddy
from Mark's arms.

Mark jerked away
from the grasping hands,
glaring.
But it was his mother
he glared at.
"There *is* somebody!"
he shouted.
"Don't you know?
I want a dog!
I *need* a dog!
I've needed a dog

my whole life!"

And having said that,
he had said it all.
There was nothing more.
So,
holding Buddy close
against his heart,
Mark turned
and ran.

42

When Mark grew too tired
to run any longer,
he walked.
When his arms grew too tired
to carry the little dog any farther,
he set Buddy down beside him.
Then he watched
to see what she would do.
She stayed close without a leash,
so they kept going.
When they reached the edge of town,
they stopped
and stood for a long time,
gazing across the fields
and the patches of shadowy woods
that stretched beyond Erthly.
A light shone
in a farmhouse
far away.
Too far away to reach by walking.
And even if he tried,
what would he say
when he got there?
"No one wants us in Erthly.

Can we come live with you?"

Mark knelt beside the little dog.
He stroked her satiny coat,
and she gazed up at him
with trusting eyes.
"I'm sorry,"
he said.
"I don't know what else to do."
And so,
still walking side by side,
they began the trek
toward
home.

Stars winked
in a clearing sky
by the time they reached Walnut Street.

When they came to Charles Larue's mansion,
the oak tree,
and the tall iron fence
with spikes,
Walnut Street stood silent and empty.
Mark checked the tower,
but he saw no one.

A few blocks on,
though,
he could see a light shining
on the front stoop
of his house.
When he got there,
when he walked up the sidewalk
with Buddy at his side,
he found his mother
sitting on the top step,
waiting.

"Hello, Mark,"
she said.

Mark's feet stopped.
Buddy stopped
beside him.

His mother stood.
"Will you come in?"
she said.

"Buddy, too?"
he asked.

"Yes,"

his mother replied.
"We can't have lost dogs
running loose
in Erthly."

Mark and Buddy followed his mother
into the house.
Mark stopped
just inside the door.
Buddy sat down neatly
by his side.

Mark checked out
the crease
in the pale space
between his mother's eyebrows,
and then
he began talking.
The words tumbled out.
"Please,"
he began.
"You've got to understand."

And so he told her
what it was like to be a boy
without a dad
or a brother

or a sister
or even a cousin
living close enough to count.
He told her how lonely their little house was
sometimes,
even when they both were there.
He even told her how,
every night,
he patted the edge of his bed
and how,
every night,
his imaginary dog
jumped up
to sleep
next to him.

His mother listened,
her gaze traveling back and forth
between Mark
and the small black and brown dog.
When Mark was done talking,
the room itself seemed to hold its breath.
Then,
just when he thought
no one
would ever speak

again,
his mother began.

She told him about a little girl
and about a big dog
with lots of teeth.
She told about being hurt,
about being scared,
about how dogs—
even small dogs
who were perfectly polite with their teeth—
still made her tremble inside.
And after she had told him all that,
she said,
"I'm sorry, Mark.
I didn't understand."

Mark melted
like butter.
His mother was afraid?
His mother,
who had brought him into the world
alone,
who had taken care of him
every day of his life
alone,

who had faced every crisis—
flu and flat tires and overflowing toilets—
alone,
his brave mother
was afraid of this small
black and brown
dog?

He took a deep breath,
then asked,
"Will you let me teach you
how to say hello
to a dog
you've never met before?"

The crease grew deeper,
but still
his mother nodded.

So Mark showed her . . .
how to speak in a soft voice,
how to put her hand out slowly
to let Buddy sniff,
how to give the little dog a scratch
on the neck.
"Polite dogs don't put their paws

on one another's heads,"
he said.

His mother scratched Buddy
very carefully,
just below her chin.
Then she smiled.
When Buddy sniffed her hand
and gave it a lick,
the smile grew.

"Mom,"
Mark said,
"please?
I need—"

"I know,"
his mother said.
And then she added,
"Miss Klein is going to bring
Buddy's things over here tomorrow.
Apparently
there is a stuffed cat
she is quite fond of."

Mark threw his arms

around his mother
and cried.

43

Mark patted the place
next to where he lay in bed.
"Here you go,"
he said.
"Come on up now."

The little dog
jumped
right
up.

Mark picked up one of her paws
and pressed the pads to his nose.
Her feet
smelled like warm toast.
He ran a finger from her narrow muzzle
all the way to her whiplike tail.
Her coat was smooth and silky warm.
What perfect ears she had!
What a nice brown mask!
What a pretty circle of brown fur

beneath her tail!
She was perfect in every way . . .
except,
maybe,
her name.
A girl dog
shouldn't be named
Buddy.
Besides . . .
a new dog
in a new home
deserved a new name.

So he said to his mother
when she came
to tuck them both in,
"Name something precious."
"You,"
she answered
without a second's thought,
and she brushed her palm
across his porcupine hair.
"Something else,"
he said.
"Diamonds,"
she said.

Mark studied the little black and brown dog,
then shook his head.
"Can you think of something else?"
he asked.
"Rubies?"
his mother offered.
Mark thought about that.
Ruby.
He liked it.
"I'm going to call her Ruby,"
he told his mother.
"What do you think?"

He said the name like someone
reciting a prayer.

"I think 'Ruby' is perfect,"
his mother told him.

Mark gave his mom a hug.
Then
he cupped Ruby's pointy face
between his hands
and kissed his dog
on the lips.

Ruby was quick.

She caught Mark's mouth with her tongue
at the exact instant of the kiss.
"Arghhh!" Mark said.
And he wiped his mouth with the back of his hand.

Then he kissed her on the lips
again.

44

Ruby rose into the air
just beneath the spinning red ball.
She rose and rose
as though her hind legs were springs,
as though her front ones were wings.
At the very top of her leap,
she snatched the ball,
twisted,
and landed neatly
on all four paws.
Lifting her head high,
lifting her paws
to dance
through the crisp carpet of leaves,
she brought the ball
to Mark,
dropped it,

shining with spit,
at his feet,
and bowed
a dog's deep let's-play-some-more bow.
"Good girl!" Mark said,
and he picked up the ball
and threw it again.

His friends would be here soon,
the Dog-Park Pack.
They would come,
as they did nearly every day,
to the dog park
with their dogs—
or their almost-dogs—
and everyone would run and play together
in the autumn sunshine.
Larue would probably come out
onto his porch
to watch
too.
(That's what he'd told the kids to call him,
just Larue.)
The town had given him
a shiny new bench for his porch,
so he could sit and watch,

so anyone who came by
could sit with him
to visit.

Ruby dropped the ball
at Mark's feet
again.
How could such a small dog
be so fast?
How could she keep those fantastic ears
flying?

Mark lunged at her to change the game,
and she took off,
running.
He followed,
splashing through the crisp leaves—
red and gold and bronze—
until he could dart behind a pine tree
and crouch there,
hidden in its fat shadow.
When Ruby discovered she was no longer
being chased,
she turned back,
sniffing
zigzag

along
the
ground
as though any scent she found there
would surely bring her
to her boy.
What kind of trail she had hold of,
Mark could only guess.
A rabbit's,
maybe,
or a night-wandering raccoon.
Perhaps the skitterings of the squirrels.
Whatever it was,
she came charging
around the base of the tree
to pounce against his chest.
Mark pretended to be bowled over,
and the two of them rolled and rolled
through the dusty crunch of leaves.
Then they lay together,
heart to heart,
panting.

Friends,
a dog park,
a mother who understood,
a dog.

What more could a boy want?

Friends,
a dog park,
a mother who understood,
a boy.
What more could a dog want
either?

Little dog,
lost.
Little black dog with brown paws
and a brown mask
and a sweet ruffle of brown fur on her bum
just beneath her black whip of a tail.
Satiny coat.
Ears like airplane wings
that drop,
just at the tips.

Little dog,
found.